BEN RICE

*Pobby and Dingan*

Ben Rice lives in London. This is his
first book.

*Pobby*
*and*
*Dingan*

# Pobby
# and
# Dingan

## BEN RICE

*Vintage Books*

*A Division of Random House, Inc.*

*New York*

FIRST VINTAGE BOOKS EDITION, APRIL 2003

The Library of Congress has cataloged the Knopf edition as follows:
Rice, Ben.
Pobby and Dingan / Ben Rice.
New York: Knopf, 2000.
p. cm.
1. Imaginary companions—Fiction.  2. Brothers and sisters—Fiction.
3. Lightning Ridge (N.S.W.)—Fiction.
PR6068.I1214 P64 2000
823'.92—dc21
00700380

Vintage ISBN: 978-1-400-03188-7

*Book design by Virginia Tan*

www.vintagebooks.com

146122990

*For Mollie*

The secret of an opal's color lies not in its substance but in its absences.

—*Australian Geographic*, 1998

*Pobby*
*and*
*Dingan*

# 1

Kellyanne opened the car door and crawled into my bedroom. Her face was puffy and pale and fuzzed-over. She just came in and said: "Ashmol, Pobby and Dingan are maybe-dead." That's how she said it.

"Good," I said. "Perhaps you'll grow up now and stop being such a fruit loop."

Tears started sliding down her face. But I wasn't feeling any sympathy, and neither would you if you'd grown up with Pobby and Dingan.

"Pobby and Dingan aren't dead," I said, hiding my anger in a swig from my can of Mello Yello. "They never existed. Things that never existed can't be dead. Right?"

Kellyanne glared at me through tears the way she did the time I slammed the door of the ute in Dingan's face or the time I walked over to where Pobby was supposed to be sitting and punched the air and kicked the air in the head to show Kellyanne that Pobby was a figment of her imaginings. I don't know how many times I had sat at the dinner table saying: "Mum, why do you have to set places for Pobby and Dingan? They aren't even real." She put food out for them too. She said they were quieter and better behaved than me and deserved the grub.

"They ain't exactly good conversationists, but," I would say.

And at other times when Kellyanne held out Pobby and Dingan were real I would just sit there saying, "Are not. Are not. Are not," until she got bored of saying, "Are. Are. Are," and went running out screaming with her hands over her ears.

And many times I've wanted to kill Pobby and Dingan, I don't mind saying it.

My dad would come back from the opal mines covered in dust, his beard like the back end of a dog that's shat all over its tail. He would be saying: "Ashmol, I sensed it today! Tomorrow we'll be on opal, son, and we'll be bloody millionaires! I can feel those bewdies sitting there in the drives, staring back at me. Checking me out. Waiting. They're red-on-blacks, Ashmol, I'll bet you anything! There's rumours going that Lucky Jes has taken out a million-dollar stone and a fossilized mammoth tooth with sun-flash in it. We're close, boy. Close. There's definitely something in that earth with the name Williamson on it!"

"Fairdinkum?"

His excitement always caught ahold of me. I would get a tingle down my neck and I would sit there with my ears pricking up like a hound's, my tongue hanging out, watching my dad's eyes darting around in his head. They were strange eyes—blue and green and with a flicker of gold in them. "Eyes like opals," my mum once said with a sigh, "only a little easier to find."

Well, while Dad was pacing around the yard brushing himself off a bit and swigging from a stubby of V.B., Kellyanne would say, "Dad, be careful! You almost trod on Pobby with your fat feet! Watch what you're doing!" But Dad would be too excited to do anything but say: "Aw, sorry, princess. Did I tread on your fairy-friends?" That was Dad. Me and him never took Pobby and Dingan seriously one bit.

But there were others who did. The older, softer sort of folks in Lightning Ridge had sort of taken to Pobby and Dingan. They had totally given up throwing Kellyanne funny looks and teasing her about them. Now when she walked down Opal Street, some of the old-timers would stop and shout: "G-day, Kellyanne, g-day, Pobby, and how's Miss Dingan doin' today?" It made you want to be sick all over the place. Lightning Ridge was full of flaming crackpots as far as I could see. It was like the sun had burnt out their brains. Now, I was as much a rockhound as the next kid, but I wasn't crazy enough to talk to imaginary friends, I'll tell you that for nothing. But one time Ernie Finch let Kellyanne enter Dingan in for the Opal Princess competition because Kellyanne had a cold. I'm not kidding. And the judges voted Dingan third place, and Nils O'Reiordan from the newspaper came and took photographs of Kellyanne with her arm around Dingan's invisible shoulder, and made out he was asking Dingan questions and everything. It was embarrassing. When the newspaper came out there was a picture of Kellyanne wearing a little silver crown over her long blond hair, and underneath there was this sentence saying: *Two Opal Princesses—Kellyanne Williamson (aged eight) and her invisible friend Dingan, who won third prize in this year's Opal Princess competition.* Plus, every time we went to Khan's, Mrs. Schwartz would hand my sister three lollies and say, "There you go, Kellyanne. One for you, one for Pobby and one for Dingan. They look like they're both doing good." Everybody knew everybody in Lightning Ridge. And some people even knew nobody as well, it seemed. Pobby and Dingan fat into that little town just fine.

"Find anything today?" Mum asked one night when she'd got back from her job on the checkout at Khan's and me and Dad were relaxing after a hard afternoon's work out at the claim.

"Potch. Nothing special."

"Nothing?"

I could see Kellyanne through the window over Dad's shoulder. She was sitting out back on a pile of stones talking to Pobby and Dingan, her mouth moving up and down, her hands waving around like she was explaining something to them. But all she was really talking to was the night and a few gallahs. And if she was honest she would have admitted it there and then. But not Kellyanne.

"Where's my little girl?" Dad asked.

"Outside playing with some friends," said my mum, fixing my dad a look straight between the eyes.

"Pobby and Dingan?"

"Yup."

My dad sighed. "Jesus! That girl's round the twist," he said.

"No she isn't," said my mum, "she's just different."

"She's a fruit loop," I said.

"I kind of wish they were real friends, Mum," Dad said. "She don't seem to get on with the other kids around here too much."

"What d'you expect?" said my mum, raising her voice and putting her hands on her hips. "What d'you bloody expect when you drag your family to a place like Lightning Ridge? What d'you bloody expect to happen when you bring up an intelligent girl like Kellyanne in a place full of holes and criminals and freaks?"

"I still say Kellyanne could do with some real-live mates," went on my dad, as if he was talking to someone inside his beer.

Mum had stomped off into the kitchen. "Maybe they *are* real!" she shouted back at him after rattling a few plates together. "Ever thought about that, ye of little bloody imagination?"

My dad pulled a face. "Who? Pobby and Dingan? Ha!" He drained his beer can, positioned it standing up on the floor and stamped on it until it was a disc of metal. Then he threw me a wink as if to say: "Here comes the next wave of the attack, Ashmol!" And it came.

"Damn, Rex! You make me so bloody angry. Honestly! You haven't found any opal in two years. Not a glimpse of it. And opal's real enough for *you*. You don't stop dreaming about it and talking in your sleep to it like a lover! Well, as far as I'm concerned your bloody opal doesn't exist either!"

But that was a stupid thing for Mum to say, because the shops were full of opal and there were pictures of it everywhere and everybody was talking about it and the Japanese buyers forked out a whole heap of dollars for it. That's a fact. I saw them doing it with my own eyes out at Hawk's Nest.

Well, after my mum said this stuff about opal and after she'd done her usual piece about there being no money left in the tin under the bed, Dad sulked around a bit and kicked a few rocks around out in the yard. But then suddenly the door swung open and he came in full of energy like a new man and with a strange smile on his face. And what did he do? He started asking Kellyanne about Pobby and Dingan and how their days had been and what they were doing tomorrow. And he had never done that before in his life, ever. But he did it in a voice so you weren't too sure if he was joking around or not. Kellyanne was studying his face carefully, trying to work him out for herself. And so was I. And so was

Mum. And then Dad asked Kellyanne if he could run Pobby and Dingan a bath. And he asked straight-faced and honest-sounding and Kellyanne eventually said yes, that was all right, but only she was allowed to dry them after it.

I said: "Dad, what the hell are you doing? You know all that Pobby and Dingan stuff's just horseshit! She'll never grow out of it if you talk like that!"

And Dad answered, looking at his feet: "No, Ashmol. I think I've been unfair on Pobby and Dingan. I think that they do exist after all! I just haven't, like, recognized it until now." He grinned and rubbed his hands together and disappeared into the bathroom to run the taps while Kellyanne stood there glowing with pride and flashing me a smile from the doorway which made me feel sick. I looked at Mum, but she had a contented look on her face and started setting about making tea and cookies. I sat at the table feeling like someone had marooned me on a desert island.

Well, I don't like thinking about it, but from that moment on my dad became a total dag. Now when he got up in the morning and woke up Kellyanne for school he would wake up Pobby and Dingan too. Yes, he would. He started talking to them like they was real people. And he wasted all kinds of money on buying them birthday presents too—good money that could have gone into a better generator if you ask me. Oh, yes, Dad had himself some fun by going along with the Pobby and Dingan thing. One time he even took

*Pobby and Dingan*

Kellyanne, Pobby and Dingan out to the Bore Baths in the ute. When I ran out to join them with my towel around my shoulders, my dad shouted: "Sorry, son. Can't take you today, Ashmol. Not enough room with Pobby and Dingan in here." He waved out of the window with a big smile on his face and drove off thinking he was a funny kind of bloke. Sometimes Mum would ask him to come and help with the washing up. But no! Dad was helping Pobby and Dingan get dressed or helping them with their homework. Kellyanne loved it. But Mum went a bit strange. I don't think she could decide if she was angry or pleased that Dad had become mates with Pobby and Dingan. And I think even Kellyanne began to realize pretty soon that Dad was only doing it to get back at Mum for having a go at him or something. He wasn't a very subtle sort of bloke, my dad, when it came down to it. He drank too much for a start and spent too much time underground in the dark.

## 2

When Dad left for the claim one morning he volun-
teered to take Pobby and Dingan with him to get some
exercise while Kellyanne was at school. He was trying
to separate her from them, I suppose, now I think about
it. Kellyanne's teachers, you see, had complained that
she wasn't concentrating in class and was always talking
to herself and hugging the air. Well, I got to admit it
was a funny sight seeing my dad heading out holding
hands with two invisible people. Kellyanne watched
him, making sure he helped them up into the cabin of
the ute, and then Dad started the car up and waved out
of the window and made out he was fastening Pobby
and Dingan's seat belts.

"Don't worry, princess!" he shouted. "I'll look after
them while you're at school and make sure they
don't get up to no mischief. Won't I, Pobby? Won't I,
Dingan?"

I was getting a bit worried. My dad was turning into a poof. And the neighbours were talking about him walking alone and talking to himself and things like that. They said he was even drunker than normal.

That same night Mum still wasn't back from work and Dad had swallowed a few beers too many, shall we say. He was singing "Heartbreak Hotel," and doing a sort of Elvis dance. I knew he had forgotten to bring back Pobby and Dingan from the claim, but I didn't say a word. I wanted to see what Kellyanne would have to say about it, so I just sat there playing on my Super Mario with its flat batteries, hoping Kellyanne would come in from the kitchen and get all ratty. Dad sat down and started talking about how he had been up at the puddling dam doing a bit of agitating. He told me that today Old Sid the Grouch had found traces of colour within twenty metres of his claim. I said: "Do your Elvis dance again, Dad, it's really cool." Of course it wasn't cool at all, but I wanted to keep him from thinking about his day. He might have remembered about Pobby and Dingan in the nick of time. Luckily he didn't and Kellyanne came rushing in from the kitchen, where she was having a go at cooking yellowbelly from Mum's instructions.

"Dad. Where's Pobby and Dingan? Where are they?" she cried, all anxious.

"Now you're in for it, Dad," I said. "Better make something up quick."

Dad's face suddenly flushed all kinds of colours. He swivelled around and spilt some beer on the floor. "Hi, princess! Relax now, darl. Pobby and Dingan's right here sittin' on the couch next to Ashmol."

Kellyanne looked over at the couch. "No they're not, Dad," she said. "They hate Ashmol. Where are they really?"

"Oh no, that's it," said my dad, "I completely forgot. They're out in the back yard watering the plants."

Kellyanne ran outside. She came back looking pale. "Dad, you forgot all about Pobby and Dingan, didn't you? You've lost them, haven't you?"

"No, princess," said my dad. "Calm down, sweetheart. They were in the ute with me when I came back."

"I don't believe you," said Kellyanne, tears growing out of her eyes. "I want you to take me out to the claim to look for them right now." That was my sister! She was mad as a cut snake.

"Christ, Kellyanne!" I said. "Grow up, girl!"

Dad looked a bit desperate. "Aw, princess, come on, now. I'm busy having a brew and a chat with Ashmol. Are you sure your little friends aren't here?"

"Positive," said Kellyanne, wiping her eyes on her sleeve.

And so Dad couldn't do nothing except take Kellyanne out to the claim called Wyoming, where he had his drives.

"You come too, Ashmol," Dad said.

"No thanks," I said, folding my arms across my chest. "Count me out. No bloody way is Ashmol Williamson going looking for two non-existent things."

But in the end I went along all the same, making sure I did lots of tutting and shaking my head.

When we arrived at the claim the two of them walked around calling out: "Pobby! Dingan! P-P-P-Pobbbbby! Where are you?" I sat firm on a mullock heap and opened up a can of Mello Yello. I knew what my dad was thinking. He was thinking that any minute now Kellyanne was going to suddenly imagine she had found her imaginary friends and start beaming all over her face. But she didn't. She kept calling out and looking real worried. She ran around the four corners of the claim looking from side to side. Pobby and Dingan were nowhere to be seen, she said. And who was going to argue with her? Dad wasn't. And I was having shit-all to do with it.

They looked behind the mullock heaps and they looked in the old Millard caravan, where we used to live when we first came out to the Ridge, and they looked behind the mining machinery and behind a clump of leopard gums. And I'll bet all the time my dad was thinking: "I must be going hokey cokey. If the other miners could see me now!" Dad knew pretty darn well, you see, that only Kellyanne was going to find Pobby and Dingan. He would just have to wait until she did. Or maybe he was secretly hoping that this was Kellyanne's little way of putting her imaginary friends

behind her for good. Anyway, he kept throwing desperate glances my way and shouting over: "Come on,
Ashmol, lend a frigging hand, will you?" But I wasn't
budging, and so eventually Dad sat down exhausted by
the hoist where the huge blower was curled up like a
snake and just called out, "Pobby! Dingan! Listen! You
two! I'm sorry I didn't look after you proper! I'm sorry I
left you out here! I've got some lollies in my pocket if
you want some!" That was a fat lie. He never had any
lollies.

Well, in the last hour before dark Dad pulled himself
off his backside and looked real hard. You had to hand it
to him. He got down on his knees and crawled around in
the dirt. He rummaged through piles of rocks. He
looked behind trees, in front of trees, up trees and down
trees. He crossed over onto the next claim, which was
owned by Old Sid the Grouch. He shouldn't of. But
he did. He searched like he was mad, and there was
sweat slipping down his cheeks. He worked harder
than he ever mined in his life, I reckon. And it was hard
to believe he was searching for Nothing. Diddlysquat.
Stuff-all. And then there was a piece of very bad
timing.

Old Sid, who lived out there in a camp made out of
pieces of corrugated iron, came running out from
behind a weeping-wilga tree and stood by the star-
picket at the corner of our claim with his arms folded.
He had a big grey moustache, and he wore this kind of
stupid beanie hat that made him look even meaner and

stupider than he was. And believe me that was stupid. The rumour was he ate frill-neck lizards on toast for breakfast.

Old Sid watched as my dad got down on all fours and leant over the hole of Old Sid's mine shaft and called out, "Pobby and Dingan! You down there?" Sid couldn't make head or tail of what was going on. He thought my dad was ratting his claim and stealing all his opal. He shouted out: "Hey! You! Rex Williamson! What the hell you doin' on my claim?"

My dad turned around, startled. He was totally off his guard. He began to go red and get all embarrassed and then he started trying to make up some sort of story about looking for his watch, but then he changed it halfway into a lost-cat story—but he stuttered over that too and so he got back down on his knees and started spinning some yarn about looking for one of his contact lenses. It all went a bit wrong. My dad wasn't much good at lying.

"You been drinking, Rex?"

I walked up to Sid to put things straight.

"My dad ain't been drinking nothing, Mr. Sid," I said. "You see, my sister's got two imaginary friends called Pobby and Dingan—maybe you've heard of them—and she thinks my dad lost them out on the claim. And we're here looking for them. Sounds strange, I know—but there you go, that's the truth of it."

Sid looked totally baffled and pretty angry. He said: "Now, don't you go making excuses for your old man, Ashmol Williamson! You may be a clever kid, but your daddy's been ratting my claim, ain't he? Some of us miners have been suspecting him for some time. But now here's the proof of it! And you're just trying to stick up for him, ain't you?"

My dad stumbled over to Old Sid with his fists clenched. He said, "Now, look here, Sid. I ain't been ratting nothing. I ain't no thief. I'm looking for my daughter's imaginary friends and you'd better bloody well believe it, mate!"

But Sid wasn't having any of it. "You can talk about invisible people as much as you like, Rex Williamson," he said. "But I've had my doubts about you. A lot of us have. I've already reported you to the mining authority, and as soon as I saw you on my claim this evening, snuffling around for my opal, the first thing I did was radio the police, and, as a matter of fact, here they are right now!"

The noise of a car drove into our ears and a four-wheel-drive police jeep came wobbling down the creamy red track that leads to our claim. It pulled over by our old Millard caravan and out came two policemen. Bulky fellas with hats and badges and shit. I was getting a bit worried. Kellyanne was still looking around the claim for Pobby and Dingan, and Dad had started shouting about how dare Old Sid call him a ratter, he who'd worked honestly for God knows how long, and been a pretty good sort of bloke all round. And then I went up to one of the police blokes and told him the truth of the matter about Pobby and Dingan and what my dad was doing on Old Sid's claim. But I hadn't got too far when there was this noise of scuffling and a grunt and I turned around to see that my dad had lost his cool and snotted Old Sid one in the nose. Well, after that the police were on my dad in a flash, and they had him in handcuffs and everything. Kellyanne came running over in a panic, saying, "Leave my dad alone! Leave him alone!" But Dad was bundled into the car and driven away in a flash. And it was us who were left alone. And then Kellyanne sat down on a mullock heap and broke down in sobs, for I reckon it was a bit too much to cope with, losing two imaginary friends and one real dad in an afternoon.

For a while I didn't know what to do. I just stood there watching one of those fluffy roly-poly things go cartwheeling over the claim on a breath of wind. And I thought about my dad and what a tangle he'd got himself into. And then I said: "Kellyanne, come on, we'd better get home. Pobby and Dingan will come back tonight on their own and Dad will be fine as soon as this is sorted out and the police realize what he was doing on Sid's land. Come on, we'll walk back and tell Mum, and get the bad bits over and done with."

But Kellyanne didn't stop looking worried. She legged it over to the mine shaft and stepped over the tape which was around the top of the hole to stop people entering. She got down on all fours and peeked over the edge. And she called out Pobby and Dingan's names down the mine shaft. There was no reply, of course. She stayed there on all fours looking down that shaft for half an hour.

"This just isn't like them," she said. "This is not like them at all."

While Kellyanne was doing this I walked over to Old Sid the Grouch, who was still watery-eyed with pain and holding on to his nose and mooching around his claim checking to see if all his opal dirt was still there. I said: "You've made a big mistake here, Mr. Sid. We Williamsons were just looking for my sister's imaginary friends. We ain't no ratters."

Old Sid spat on the ground and said something about our family needing our heads inspected, and how my poor mother was too much of a pom for this place, and how he felt sorry for us that our dad was a ratter, and how the rumour was my dad had come to the Ridge in the first place to hide away from the law. And I felt so angry I walked right away, pulled Kellyanne up by the arm and marched her home. It took an hour and a half, and all the way Kellyanne was whining about how she'd lost Pobby and Dingan, and how she wouldn't be able to sleep or eat until she found them, and how if they'd been there then they could have saved Dad and none of this would have happened. Her worried little face was covered in white dust so she looked like a little ghost.

Well, it was dark when we got back to our home, and my mum had already heard what had happened from the police and she sent us to bed and said not to worry because everything would be sorted out soon. But I never saw her looking so angry and panicky and unsorted-out in her life. And her bedroom light stayed on all night, I swear.

And that night at around twelve was when Kellyanne crawled into my bedroom through the Dodge door which I'd got Dad to fix up to make going to bed more interesting. And my sister looked at me all pale and fuzzy-faced and said: "Ashmol, Pobby and Dingan are maybe-dead." And she just sat there in her pyjamas all nervous and hurt. But I was half thinking of Dad and if he was in prison and how the whole thing was Pobby and Dingan's fault. And then I tried to get my head round how it could be their fault if they didn't even exist.

And I fell asleep thinking about that.

# 3

When I woke up the next day, Mum told me how Dad had been in prison overnight but he was being released and sent home until there was a trial or something which would prove that Dad hadn't been ratting Old Sid's claim. Mum was pretty frantic with worry, though, and she said Dad would have to keep a low profile in the Ridge and stay at home a while, until the whole thing had blown over and he'd got his respect back amongst all the miners and stuff. Ratting, you see, is the same thing as murder in Lightning Ridge—only a bit worse.

We waited for him to come home and played a game of chess to help pass the time and calm each other down. I got Mum in checkmate after fifteen moves. No one can beat me at chess, and I reckon one day I'll be a bloody grandmaster or something. Either that or a secret agent like James Blond. But I have to admit that this time Mum wasn't concentrating too well and so she made it pretty easy for my bishops and knights to do the business. The problem was that Mum kept gazing out of the window with a dazed look about her, and I was pretty sure she wasn't just thinking about Dad but she was also pommie-sick again and thinking about Granny Pom and the other pommie friends she left behind her in England all those years ago.

Anyway, when Dad eventually came home late that afternoon he gave us all a hug and said that the prison was okay and a bit like a motel except that the beds were hard and the bars weren't the kind that served beer. He said not to worry, because he was going to sort out this whole mess good and proper. But he didn't know quite how. And Mum told him he'd better not try and sort out anything but just keep his head down and keep out of trouble until the trial and all that shit. And then my dad asked me if Pobby and Dingan had come back yet. I shook my head. "Kellyanne thinks they are maybe-dead," I said.

"She's still very upset," said my mum. "She's been sulking all day. You shouldn't have been so careless, Rex, you really shouldn't."

"I shouldn't have done a lot of things," said my dad, letting out a long sigh. But he was pleased to be back. And he was glad I think of all the attention we were giving him. I even went and got him a stubby of V.B. from the fridge and then I sat there asking him more things about prison. And after that we talked about opal all day, until it got dark and until there was suddenly this godawful shriek and Mum came rushing in from near

the front door saying, "Oh, my Lord! God! Help! Get
water! Get water fast!" She ran into the kitchen and
started filling up a bucket from the sink.

We rushed out front and what hit me first was a
smokey smell like the smell of a cigar. And then, when I
peered out into the dark, I could see grey figures twist-
ing up into the sky quite awesomely. Dancing. But my
dad whispered: "Jesus! They've set our fence on fire!"
And then I twigged that those figures were swirls of
smoke, and some of the stakes were actually flaming at
the tops. The light from the flame danced against the
walls of our little house and showed up enormous dark
lines like zebra stripes. They were letters sprayed on
with an aerosol can or something, and they said:

BURN THE RATTERS

Mum threw her bucket of water over the fence post
while I ran in to fill up some more and Dad just stood
gaping at the words on the wall beside the living-room
window. He was there when I came back, still staring,
his hand on the back of his neck, not saying a word.
And then he disappeared around the back of our house
for paint. When the flames were out I went into
Kellyanne's room and told her what had happened. But
she just hid under her blanket and said nothing.

# 4

About this time Kellyanne started getting really sick. I can't explain it and neither could anybody else. She just lay in bed saying that she was very tired and worried because Pobby and Dingan hadn't come back, and that she couldn't be sure if they were dead or not. They might still be wandering around over the opal fields all lost and frightened, and there were wild pigs out there and snakes and all kinds. It made her want to puke just to think about it. Well, Pobby and Dingan had got us into enough shit as it was, thank you very much, and I felt angry with them. Pretty goddamn angry for spoiling our family name. And I thought Kellyanne was faking at first, pretending to be ill like she pretended to have friends. But then I heard her puking in the dunny. She *was* sick. She really was.

She wouldn't eat anything. Mum called Jack the Quack and he came and sat on Kellyanne's bed and did some stethoscope stuff. He told my mum that Kellyanne was suffering from a nervous illness or depression, and that she had a fever. He tried to persuade her to eat a little of something. But she wouldn't. He told Kellyanne that if she kept this up he would have to take her to hospital and force-feed her through some disgusting pipes. I told Jack about everything that had happened with Pobby and Dingan but he just smiled and frowned and smiled again and used the words "syndrome" and "clinical" and "psychological" a lot. Well, I didn't know what those words meant but they sounded like pretty useless kinds of words to me.

Before Jack the Quack left he hung around talking to Dad about his new jackhammer. He told him that he'd heard about the scuffle out at the claim and that he was behind Dad all the way—and didn't believe a word of the rumours that were spreading around Lightning Ridge like a bushfire. But there was something funny about how Jack the Quack was behaving. Sort of nervousish. And when he said Kellyanne would be better off in hospital, I reckoned he said that because he didn't trust my folks to look after her. Plus, when Mum asked him to stay for dinner he made some excuse about having to go line-dancing and scuttled away like a goanna.

My dad started to look pale too. He said, "No bastard's taking my princess to no stupid hospital," over and over again. "We Williamsons can look after each other just fine. We don't need no charity or help from nobody!" Late at night he would pace up and down, shaking his head, saying: "You're right, Mum. This is all my fault. Maybe we should never have come out to the Ridge in the first place. She's a sensitive kid. Too precious for this place. She gets bullied at school, don't she?" That was my dad. He started to get all emotional, and cracked open tinny after tinny of V.B. And then he cried. It was like the beer was going in his mouth and coming out of his eyes.

Well, Mum and Dad didn't dare tell Kellyanne to stop this once and for all or explain to her straight that Pobby and Dingan were only in her imagination and that she'd better switch the bloody thing off. They'd done it once before, you see, and Kellyanne went a little bit crazy and started screaming so hard the whole town thought they was being air-raided by nuclear missiles from France. They knew better than to tell my sis that she was being stupid. Kellyanne didn't handle that kind of criticism stuff too well.

So now Kellyanne just lay in bed. She slept or just lay whimpering. That's all that she did. She got so thin that it didn't look like there was any kind of body under the sheet.

Well, all this started to rattle my mind, and every day I would wriggle through the car door and clamber up on to my bunk and sit thinking. I figured this was the end of the world, because we were all going crazy. Pobby and Dingan were messing up my family and they weren't even here. And they also weren't even anywhere. And although I thought my sister was nuts, I didn't like to see her like this and hear her chucking up in the dunny.

And I wanted my dad to cheer up and go off to his mining again, and I wanted my mother to stop worrying and being homesick, and I wanted the Williamson family name to gleam and sparkle and be all right.

And I knew flaming well that the answers to all these problems lay with Pobby and Dingan themselves.

And then I figured out something else. I didn't like to admit it, but it seemed to me the only way to make Kellyanne better would be to find Pobby and Dingan. But how do you go looking for imaginary friends? I stayed awake all the bastard-night trying to get my head around the problem. I reckoned that the first thing would be to have as many people as possible looking for them, or pretending to look, so that at least Kellyanne knew that people cared, that they believed in her imaginary friends and wanted to help out. See, I'd remembered that Kellyanne was always most happy when people asked questions about Pobby and Dingan. Usually that made a smile crawl over her face. And it seemed to me if a hell of a lot of people was asking questions about them then she would get better fast. I also knew darn well that there was quite a few people in the Ridge who loved Kellyanne to bits even though they were a little unsure about the rest of us Williamsons, and there were some who almost believed in Pobby and Dingan or who were real nice and understanding about it. And I had it in the back of my mind that if those people believed in imaginary friends and all that shit, or if they knew how real those friends were for Kellyanne, then they'd believe that my dad really had been looking for them out at the mine and not ratting Old Sid's claim.

The two problems seemed to go together somehow. So this is what I did. The next day I went around town calling in at the shops and telling people why Kellyanne was sick. I went to The Wild Dingo, and even to The Digger's Rest, where the toughest miners drink. I said, "Howdy, I'm Ashmol Williamson, and I've come to tell you my dad's no ratter and my sister's sick cos she's lost her imaginary friends." Well, there was a silence and then one of those miners came up to me, grabbed my collar and held me up by it, so that my feet came off the ground. He pulled me so close I could smell his stinking breath and said: "Listen here, kid. You go back and tell your daddy, if he ever shows his face in here again *he's* gonna be the *imaginary one*. Understand? Imaginary! Geddit? Dead!" Well, I was just about to shit myself when a bunch of other miners came over and said to the bloke, "Put the kid down, mate. Rex Williamson is a friend of mine and those kids of his are good kids." Well, this bastard threw me on the floor and said, "You wanna watch who your friends are!" to the men, and then walked out. The group of miners picked me up, brushed me down and asked if I was okay. I told them yes, but I was a little bit worried about my sister Kellyanne, because she was really sick and might get taken away to hospital, and how I was gonna try and lick clean my dad's name until it shone red on black.

I had a busy day, all rightee. I went to the Bowling Club to tell the pokie players and also to the Wallangalla Motel, where there was some line-dancing practice going on. You should of seen me. I tried to go up to people on the dance floor and get them to stop dancing and listen, but they were too busy doing their moves to the music and I kept getting caught up between people's arms. In the end I just walked up to the bloke with the tape decks and grabbed the microphone and shouted: "Ladies and gents! Sorry to interrupt your dancing, but my name's Ashmol Williamson, and my sister is sick and we need to help her find her imaginary friends tomorrow!" There was this nasty high-pitched screech from the microphone, like it didn't exactly enjoy what I'd said, and then everyone, about fifty people in all, stopped dancing and turned around and looked at me all at once. There was a silence and then I heard people mutter my dad's name and whisper the word "ratter" to each other, and some of them frowned at me, and I knew all of a sudden what it feels like to be a mosquito. Well, I coughed into the microphone and explained in a shaky voice about my sister and Pobby and Dingan and how my dad got into trouble on Old Sid's claim. And I told them how Pobby and Dingan had liked nothing better than line-dancing, and that unless we found them they might never be able to do it ever again. And then I suddenly ran out of things to say and felt a bit weird with all those lines of people looking at me, so I just put down the microphone and ran out and got back on my Chopper and pedalled off wobbly-legged.

I went almost everybloodywhere. I went to the Automobile Graveyard and spoke to Ronnie, who recognized me from the time he gave me the cool door off the Dodge. I went out to the camps at Old Chum and Vertical Bill's and the Two Mile. And some people whispered to each other about Dad and some didn't. And some folks thought I was nuts. And some were nuts themselves anyway so it didn't make no difference. I even went out and told the tourists out at the Big Opal. They patted me on the head and smiled and whispered to each other in funny languages. One big American man filmed me with his video camera and told me to say something cute into it so he could show his friends back home. But when it came to the crunch I couldn't say anything and I didn't feel too much like smiling. So I showed him my James Blond 007 impression, where I turn sharp and fire a gun like on the video that my friend Brent's parents gave him after they struck opal out at the Three Mile. And I told this tourist how when I grew up I might have a James Blond gun and everything. But then I realized I was wasting time and Kellyanne was sick, and my dad was being called a ratter, and these tourists wouldn't really give a shit, but.

I went out to the town hall, where some of the black kids were practising a traditional Korobo-something dance with their teacher in funny outfits and didgeridoos and drums. I stood there for a while and watched them and had a good laugh at how dumb they looked. And then one of them started running straight at me with a spear and told me he was going to shove it up my ass unless I dooried right off out of the hall. But the teacher stopped him and honked on her didgeridoo and told him to shut up and get back to doing his hunting dance. But before they started the dance I managed to squeeze in a few words about how sick Kellyanne was, and I also asked them if maybe they could do a dance to conjure up Pobby and Dingan some time tomorrow. And the teacher said that they would certainly think about it if they had time, and then she started going off on one about how her ancestors believed opals were dangerous and stuffed full of evil spirits, and how maybe my family was paying the price for worshipping it and drilling horrible holes in the beautiful aboriginal land.

Well, I'd had enough of hearing this goddamned hooey, as my dad called it, and so I shot off and cycled out on the dirt roads around about a couple of hundred more camps on my rusty old Chopper bike telling people about Kellyanne and how she was ill because of losing her imaginary friends. It was a hot day, and hard work, and so I made sure I was tanked up with Mello Yello to stop my mouth getting dry from all that explaining I was doing. When I told people what had happened to my sis, some of them looked at me like I was a total fruit loop. But a lot of them already knew about Pobby and Dingan, because they had kids who went to the same school as Kellyanne, out at Walgett, and they had seen her talking to them on the old school bus. One older girl out at the caravan park came up to me and said: "Are you Kellyanne Williamson's brother? My mum says you Williamsons are stupid people and your dad's a drunk ratter and so you better go away or I'll punch you the way I punched your sister that time at the Bore Baths." I gave her the finger and pedalled off fast cos she was too big for me. But she called after me: "The only friends you Williamsons have are imaginary ones! Just you remember that, Ashmol Williamson!"

But some people were real nice about it. On one of the camps a woman gave me a Mello Yello and a cake and asked me how my mum was doing at the supermarket. She said: "The sooner they get your pretty little sister to hospital the better." I answered: "Yup. But it's more complicated than that, Mrs. Wallace. See, Kellyanne's sick-with-worry sick; she ain't hospital-sick sick." I also met this kid who knew as much about Pobby and Dingan as I did. He said he didn't like Kellyanne too much but he thought Pobby and Dingan were all right. He said he had a much better imaginary friend than Kellyanne. It was a giant green ninja platypus called Eric. He didn't talk to it, but.

One twinkly and crazy old-timer with a parrot took me into the bust-up old tram where he lived and told me he had heard Kellyanne talking to Pobby and Dingan once when she was at the town goat races. She had been standing with three lollies on Morilla Street. This old miner said he believed that Pobby and Dingan really existed and he would look out for them as carefully as he could when he was walking around town. He would also check in at Steve's Kebabs to see if they'd stopped by for a feed, and he would write a poem called "Come Home, My Transparent Ones!" and hand it around his bush-poet mates. This old codger didn't seem to understand that I just wanted him to pretend to be looking for Pobby and Dingan. But there you go.

I stayed out till dark explaining to all these Lightning Ridge families how they had to make a big show of looking for Pobby and Dingan so that Kellyanne could see that people really cared about them. And I did some explaining about what had happened to my dad and what a mix-up there had been. And how Pobby and Dingan weren't real but Kellyanne thought they were and that's what counts, and how my dad wasn't a ratter but people thought he was and that's what counts too. Some of the people were real nice about it and gave me some bags of Twisties, and I went around munching them and putting up signs I had made saying:

LOST! HELP!
KELLYANNE WILLIAMSON'S FRIENDS POBBY AND
DINGAN. DESCRIPTION: IMAGINARY. QUIET.
REWARD IF FOUND

And I put on the address of our house and tacked the notices up on telephone poles and walls and machinery and shit. When I cycled home I watched people looking at the notices, and I saw that some of them had been graffitied-over with the word "Ratter," but I also noticed that a lot of them hadn't been. Well, that was a good sign. And a lot of folks were smiling and laughing. I went to bed that night pretty full of myself for having had a go at least at clearing my family name and standing up for everybody. And I hadn't got beaten up or anything, either—which was cool.

Well, Kellyanne wasn't getting any better and she wasn't saying anything except muttering the names of Pobby and Dingan, and Mum and Dad were spending all their time by her bedside taking her temperature and telling her everything was going to be all right and making her soup which she never ate. And Dad was still pacing up and down clutching at this letter from the hospital which said that Kellyanne had to go there immediately, and that they needed to do some tests. My folks, I reckon, were beginning to think hospital was the only way out.

When the blanket everybody calls night was tucked in all snugly over Lightning Ridge I stayed in my room and hung my head out of the window and said a sort-of-a-prayer. I said something like: "Please let people go looking for Pobby and Dingan!" And I squeezed my hands together. When I'd finished the prayer, I realized I hadn't put no address on it, and I was just whispering, "P.S. This prayer is for God or anyone powerful who can hear me," and wondering if it wouldn't be better to pray to someone cooler like James Blond, when I was distracted by the sound of Mum and Dad shouting at each other in their bedroom. And I only caught a few words, because it sounded muffled, like they was shouting with bits of cake in their mouths. But I heard Mum say she was tired a lot and homesick for England and Granny Pom and fed up of working at the checkout at Khan's and not being able to look after her family for herself. And then I heard my dad shouting something about Her Royal Highness, and he kept repeating a man's name, but I can't remember what it was exactly. Probably some bloke who'd called Dad a ratter again and got him all upset and irritable.

# 5

The next day I got up early, gobbled my breakfast, attached bits of cardboard to my spokes with clothes-pegs and rode into town in fourth gear, sounding like a motorbike. There was no streams of trucks driving out early in the morning, and no sounds of the drilling rigs going at all. It seemed like the whole town had stopped mining or something. Then, just as I was going down Opal Street, I saw that there was a bunch of people crouched down on the roadside looking under bushes and cars and over fences and everything. When they saw me riding by on my souped-up Chopper, some of the people saluted me like I was some sort of general and shouted out: "Young Ashmol! Go tell Kellyanne we're searching as hard as we can!" I almost fell off my bike with surprise. The first part of my plan had worked. People were actually looking for Pobby and Dingan, they really were! I pedalled home like a maniac to tell my family.

When Dad heard what I'd gone and done he patted me on the head and said: "Good thinking, son." I told him it was important that Kellyanne saw what was taking place and Dad managed to persuade her to get out of bed. He lifted Kellyanne up in her sheet and took her out to the ute. Mum drove, because Dad wasn't comfortable about going out and being seen by people yet.

I sat in the back watching everything, and when I got into town I made Mum pull over so Kellyanne could see the special notices I had put up on the fences and gates and trees. She smiled a little when she saw them. I said, "Sorry, Kellyanne. I didn't know how to describe them proper. I mean, what do they look like?" And Kellyanne whispered that they didn't look like anything in particular, but Dingan had a lovely opal in her bellybutton, only you had to be a certain kind of person to see it. And Pobby had a limp in his right leg.

There were now lines of people all over the dirt roads, and people out with their dogs, and we pulled up alongside them and waved out of the windows. They came up to the ute and said: "Hey, Kellyanne, we've been looking for six hours now and we're not giving up until we find Pobby and Dingan. So don't worry your head about it." My sis smiled weakly. One boy asked her: "Do Dobby and Pingan speak Australian?"

"No," said my sis, "they speak English quietly. And they likes to whistle. But you have to be a certain kind of person to hear them." It was the first time Kellyanne had done this much speaking for a long while and it brought a look of hope to my mum's face.

Well, everywhere we drove we saw little groups of people out and about hunting or pretending to hunt around the trees. I saw some of the line-dancers had a banner saying *Pobby and Dingan Search Party*. One big black bloke was standing on a mullock heap looking through a pair of binoculars. I recognized he was the man who brought Kellyanne home one time when his son kicked her in the shin and pulled her long hair when they were playing out behind the service station. Dad called him "the good coon" because he was dead-crazy about opals, and one time I'd seen him doing a traditional mating dance at the wet–T-shirt competition. When we drove up in the ute he came over and poked his head through the window on Kellyanne's side and did a big grin and said: "Don' worry, girl. I'll find Pobby and Dingan in a flash for ya. I ain't Lightning Dreaming for nothing. I'm gonna go walkabout 'til I find them." And then he walked off into the bush. After that I didn't see him again for weeks, but.

Well, I think Kellyanne was pretty amazed by all this, because her eyes were wide open. She turned and whispered to me: "Are all these people looking for Pobby and Dingan?"

"That's right," I said. "Even the abos."

Kellyanne didn't say anything after that. We took her back home and she went to sleep a little more peacefully. But when Jack the Quack came around later in the evening my mum was in floods of tears. I knew then that he must have told her that my little sis was really very ill and that my plan to make her feel better had failed. I went and hid in my room, feeling like there was a rock in my throat.

My dad went walkabout that night. I heard him leaving. He was sniffing and sobbing and breathing heavy like a kettle.

# 6

I woke up in the middle of the night all restless. I got out of bed, pulled open my car door and slid out of the room. A light was on in the living room and my mum was sitting on the floor with her back towards me and her chin resting on her knee. I tiptoed up to her and saw she had something rectangleish in her hand. "What you looking at, Mum?" I asked.

My mum almost blasted off like a rocket. She jumped up onto her feet and turned around to face me all in one move. She was holding her hands out in a weird kind of karate chop. But when she saw it was me she calmed down and stopped trembling. She said: "Hey, Ashmol! It's you! Not sleepy?" I noticed she had put the thing she was holding behind her back.

"What were you looking at, Mum?" I said.

Colour went over her cheeks like rolling-flash. "Oh. It's just a photograph, Ashmol."

"Mind if I see? I really need something to knacker-out my eyes so as I can sleep."

Mum paused for a while, and then handed me the photograph with a trembling hand and sat back down on the floor. I sat down opposite her, cross-legged. The photograph was of four people standing in a line with their arms around each other. Two blokes and two women. Behind them was a sort of a hill with trees on it and the side of a building. And the hill was covered with purple dots. The sky was a mixture of blue patches and very bulging sorts of grey clouds. But the most amazing thing about the photo was the purple dots.

"What are those?" I asked, pointing at the dots.

"Bluebells," said Mum. "It's a photograph taken in England, Ashmol."

"And who're those guys in the line?" I asked, scanning over their faces. The girls were very pretty and the blokes looked smart and rich and totally into themselves. And the blokes had expensive black suits and sharp noses, and the sheilas had flowers in their hair and pale skin and dresses like they wear at the Opal Princess competition.

"That's me, Ashmol," said my mum, in a whisper. "Aged nineteen. In Granny Pom's paddock before the Castleford Ball."

"What?" I said. "Which one?" And I looked again at the photo and saw her immediately. But she looked so different it was amazing. Much sparklier and cleaner in the photograph. Slimmer and with longer hair, but not as pretty as now, that's for sure. And then I noticed one of the blokes was holding his face next to my mum's, and was looking at her real close, and his hand was on her bare shoulder.

"Who's that bloke?"

"Which one?"

"That one." I pointed to the man in the photograph with the side parting and the hand.

"Peter Sidebottom."

"Peter what?"

"Peter Juvenal Whiteway Sidebottom."

"That's a funny sort of a name," I said. "Was he a mate of yours?"

"Yes. He was." My mum paused and did her long-look-out-of-the-window thing. "He was my boyfriend before I met your father, as a matter of fact," she said.

"Oh," I said, a bit embarrassed and not sure what to say next. "Did he know the Queen?"

My mum laughed. "You're a funny boy, Ashmol! What do you mean: *Did he know the Queen?*"

"Well, he looks sort of rich," I said, "and like he might know the royal family and go shopping with them or something," I said.

"No. He didn't know the Queen," said my mum. "But you're right, Ashmol. He was rich. Well, his parents were, anyway. Now he's left England and gone to live in a place called New York in America."

I felt a bit hot under the hair and I sort of didn't want to be in the room any more. But my legs weren't going nowhere and my mouth was still wanting to talk.

"Mum, were you going to marry this Juvenile Sidebottom?" I asked.

My mum thought long and hard about this one and then said: "Perhaps. But that was before your father swept me off my feet." I felt sort of sick inside when I heard this.

"I bet that Juvenile Sidebottom's a total dag," I said. "And I bet he's not half as happy in New York as we are here at the Ridge."

"Are you happy here at the Ridge, Ashmol?" my mum asked, not taking her eyes off herself and Peter Sidebottom in the photo.

"Sure as hell am," I said, forcing out a big smile. "And you want to know why? Because here there's always opal waiting to be found, and there's always something to dream about, like another Fire Bird or a Christmas Beetle or a Southern Princess or an Aurora Australis."

"Well, yes, I suppose that's true," said my mum a little sadly.

"And I reckon my dad is going to find something real special pretty soon," I went on, "because he may not have been first in line when the money got handed out, and he may have rocks in his head, and he may have the rough end of the pineapple at the moment, but he's a pretty amazing sort of a dad all in all." Well, then I stood up and walked back towards the door, but before I went out I said, "One thing's for sure, I'm bloody glad I ain't called Ashmol Juvenile Sidebottom!" Then I walked out of the living room and closed the door behind me, and I heard my mum call out in a wobbly voice: "Good night, Ashmol Williamson! See you in the morning, hey?"

# 7

The next day people came up to our camp saying they had found Pobby and Dingan. When I made my plan I hadn't reckoned people would actually claim they had found the imaginary friends and come for their reward. The trouble was I hadn't got a reward to reward them with, because I hadn't thought that far ahead. I always just sort of thought Kellyanne would find Pobby and Dingan by herself when she realized other people were taking an interest, like. But no. At nine o'clock in the morning Fat Walt, who owned the house-made-completely-from-bottles, came and knocked on the door, calling out: "Hey, little Kellyanne Williamson! I got yer Pobby and Dingan right here wi' me!" He strode in holding his arms outstretched like he was carrying a bundle of dirty washing or something. I looked at him with a doubtful expression, knowing it wasn't going to work. "Found them out at Coocoran, I did," he said proudly.

I led him through to Kellyanne's bedroom. I said: "Kellyanne! Fat Walt's here! Says he's found Pobby and Dingan."

Kellyanne opened her eyes and I helped her sit up.

Fat Walt came through into the bedroom. "Here they are, Kellyanne," he said. "They're asleep. I found them out at Coocoran. They was shooting roos and they must have dozed off under a tree."

Kellyanne closed her eyes again and pulled up the covers. "Stop pretending," she said. "You haven't got Pobby and Dingan there, anyone can see that. Pobby and Dingan don't sleep and they don't shoot. They're pacifists. You've got nothing in your arms but thin air, and you know it."

Walt looked defeated. He said something like, "Well, have it your way, then, you little Williamson brat!" and walked out. I felt sort of sorry for him all in all.

An hour later the legendary Domingo from the castle came in all excited, mopping his forehead with a cloth. His hands were all blistered from all that lugging of rocks and castle-building he had been doing and he wore a pair of boots and blue socks pulled up to his knees. He yelled, "Hey, you fellas! You'll never guess what I found roaming around the dungeon in my castle, all lost and bewildered? Yup—your friends Pobby and Dingan. They said they'd walked twenty miles back from some opal fields. Well, you can relax now, mate, because Domingo has found them and now I've come to claim my reward. They're back at the castle waiting to be collected."

"What did Pobby and Dingan say when you found them?" asked Kellyanne in her weak little voice.

Domingo thought carefully and scratched at his chin, and said, "Hmm, well, they said they were very relieved and they wanted to see their best friend, Kellyanne Williamson, and have a big meal of steak and chips, because they were bloody starving."

"No they didn't," said Kellyanne. "Pobby and Dingan only eat Cherry Ripes and Violet Crumbles and lollies."

Domingo looked a mite desperate. "Maybe they've outgrown them now," he said. You had to give him points for quick thinking. But Kellyanne wasn't having any of it. She rolled over in her bed saying, "I wish people would stop making up such stupid stories about finding Pobby and Dingan. This whole town is going crazy. They should go back to their mines. I need to get some more sleep."

I led Domingo out, saying I was real sorry and thanks for trying at least, and he sloped off back to his half-built castle shrugging his shoulders and kicking at the dirt, saying, "Seems to me she doesn't want to find them at all." I was worried he was also thinking: "I reckon Rex Williamson's a ratter." But anyway he shook my hand and went off to work on his turrets and to wait for his dream princess to arrive on her flying horse.

All in all about ten people came that day claiming they had found Pobby and Dingan. One old lady turned up with a little jar saying she had caught them in it. Ken from the chemist's came in all stooped over saying he was giving Dingan a piggyback. He made out he had found her with a broken leg. He said he hadn't found Pobby yet but would go back to the same place he found Dingan and have a scout around. Joe Lucas, who won the log-throwing competition the year before, reckoned he found Pobby and Dingan drunk in his grandpa's wine cellar. He spent about twenty minutes doing this conversation thing in front of Kellyanne to try and make her laugh. He pretended to be trying to keep Pobby and Dingan under control and cracked lots of good jokes. A girl called Venus turned up with her Alsatian saying her dog had sniffed out the imaginary friends. Even the little boy with the Eric-the-ninja-platypus came along, claiming that his own imaginary friend had found my sister's friends. He reckoned it was only possible for imaginary friends to be found by other imaginary friends. He did the best job of all of them. But at the end of the day Eric and him were sent away with their tails between their legs. Kellyanne said that there was no way Pobby and Dingan would come back with a giant ninja platypus, because giant ninja platypuses don't exist. Anyone knows that.

# 8

Well, for a day or so all this action perked up Kellyanne a bit. It perked Lightning Ridge up too, I reckon. People around here like to get ahold of weird things, and they got so involved with the idea of Pobby and Dingan and my sister Kellyanne that they seemed to forget about Dad and Old Sid the Grouch for a while. And no one had tried to burn down our fence recently either. But even though everyone was giving her plenty of attention, Kellyanne still wasn't eating. She really did think that Pobby and Dingan had died now, and all she could talk about was bringing their corpses back. She said she'd feel plenty better if she could just be with their dead bodies. But bodies still need finding. I was getting a bit impatient with all this and so I said: "Kellyanne, you're worrying Mum and Dad sick. Everyone's trying to help, but you know damn well that you're the only one that's ever going to find Pobby and Dingan or Pobby and Dingan's bodies or whatever. Now, either find them or forget about them so you can get better and we can go back to normal!"

Kellyanne looked like she was thinking this one over and over. Eventually my sister said, "Ashmol. Please can you go out one more time to Wyoming and go down the mine. I've got a hunch about it. A sort of a feeling."

"What? You want me to go down the mine looking for Pobby and Dingan?"

"Please. And go alone and at night so that people won't be able to see you, and you won't get into trouble."

"You think they'll be there?"

"Like I said, I've got a hunch." She put her head on the pillow and pulled the blanket up to her chin. "Maybe they got lost in the drives and their bodies are still lying there in the dark all starved."

"Supposing I go," I said. "How will I know it's them? I can't *see* Pobby and Dingan like you can. Never could."

Kellyanne didn't answer. She had fallen asleep, and her arm was thin and deathly-looking. There were rings under her eyes and her face was the colour of shin-cracker.

# 9

So that night I got dressed into warm clothes and took a sausage from the fridge and put it in my pocket. I could hear Mum and Dad talking in their room in murmurs. I also got a ball of string out of the garage. I crept out of our camp and tiptoed over to where I keep my bike lying down in the dirt. I pushed it out of the drive so it didn't clank too much. And then I tied my little pocket torch to the handlebars with a bootlace and started the long journey out to the Wyoming claim. My heart was beating so hard it was like someone was pedalling inside of me.

When I was half the way out to Wyoming I stopped and asked myself what the hell I was doing going looking in the middle of the night for two dead people who didn't exist. It seemed like a pretty stupid thing for a kid to be doing. I almost made up my mind to turn around and go back, pretending I'd found the corpses of Pobby and Dingan straight away. But I knew Kellyanne wouldn't believe me. So I decided just to go and have a look down the mine shaft, and hang out there for an hour or so, so that at least I could say I'd been down and done my best. I thought Kellyanne would appreciate that. And she'd think I'd come a long way since the days when I used to punch the air where Pobby and Dingan were supposed to be. And I didn't want her to die thinking I was the kind of Ashmol who didn't believe anything.

It was a good ten clicks of cold road to the claim, and once I got off onto the dirt tracks it became harder to see where the hell I was going. I had to weave my way in and out of the burs and bindies. Luckily I sort of knew the way across the wheat paddock to the Wyoming claim blindfolded, because I'd been out there so many times with Dad. But I still had to guide my bike along the tracks without going down any potholes or knocking into any rocks. It was scary, though, being out there on my own, and so, to brave me up a bit, I kept pretending to be James Blond and I made myself a Colt .45 revolver out of two fingers and a cocked-back thumb and held it down by the leg of my trousers as I rode along. I swear for about fifteen minutes I almost forgot I was Ashmol Williamson altogether.

Well, it was now so quiet that I could hear the blood in my head creeping around and my teeth chattering together. Plus—there was this huge sky with stars peppered all over it, and I remembered Dad telling me that for each star in the sky there was an opal in the earth, and that opals are hidden from view because they are even prettier than stars and the sight of a whole lot of them would break people's hearts. And I also remembered him telling me that all this land where Lightning Ridge is now was once covered by seawater and how all kinds of sea creatures had been found fossilized in the rock. I felt a shiver go down my spine just thinking about how strange this was, that a sea was once here where now there is nothing but dry land. And suddenly I thought how maybe if this amazing thing was true it was just possible Pobby and Dingan were true too. But then I told myself: "Jesus, mate, you're losing your marbles, you fruit loop. Snap out of it." And that made me bike a little faster towards my dad's opal claim.

When I got there I undid my torch and turned it off. I laid down my Chopper and tiptoed off carefully, because I was worried that Old Sid might wake up and think I was ratting his claim. See, ever since my dad punched him in the face for calling him a ratter everyone knew that Sid stayed up late with a candle burning in his caravan, eating his frill-neck lizards and holding a gun out of his window. And I also knew he had bought a guard dog, which was why I put a sausage in my pocket.

Sure enough, Sid's dog ran out barking. He was attached to Sid's caravan by a rope. I threw him the sausage and crept over to our mine, taking care not to trip on the star-picket or fall down any holes that had been left uncovered. I heard that dog slobbering in the dark. When I got to the mine shaft I remembered how my dad would always say, "Always put your lid on when you go underground, kiddo!"—and so I tiptoed over to our old caravan and took out a yellow mining helmet from underneath it. I put on the hat and tightened the strap up under my chin. And that made me feel a little better. Then I tied my torch to my belt by the bootlace.

The mine shaft was narrow and dark. I lowered myself down carefully onto the ladder. There was only enough room on each rung for my toes, and so I had to grip extra hard onto the sides with my hands as I climbed down, in case I lost some footing. Normally my dad came down with a cord and a light-bulb thing that's attached to the generator, but all I had was my little one-battery torch, which didn't let off too much light.

One foot after the other I went down backwards, trying not to think about how I would end up if I fell. After every five steps I took a breather to make sure I was still alive and on the ladder and not at the bottom in a heap. And the further I went down the more I felt like I was in some throat, being swallowed by some monster.

Well, pretty soon my foot was on the bottom rung and I was standing on the floor of the ballroom. It felt like I was still on the ladder, because I could feel where the rungs had been pressing into my feet.

Before I set off into the darkness I remembered the story Kellyanne had told me from her *Book of Heroes and Legends* about a Greek bloke who went into an opal mine to kill a giant huntsman spider, and how he took a ball of wool so he could follow it back out and not get lost in the drives. And that's why I'd packed a ball of string and I tied it to the bottom rung of the ladder and went off down the drive. I was concentrating so damn hard on what I was doing that I nearly forgot why I had come in the first place.

I set off across the ballroom flashing my torch around and being careful not to walk into any props. The light of my torch lit up the red clay. I kept thinking I could see weird, wrinkly faces looking at me from the walls. And the further I went the more the faces became faces of people I knew or had heard something about. And one of those faces was like Old Sid's and one was Jack the Quack and one was the bloke with the stinking breath who almost clobbered me at the Digger's Rest. And one was Peter Juvenile Sidebottom. I put my mind off all these faces by saying out loud, "Sandstone and clay. Sandstone and clay. Sandstone and clay," over and over again just to remind myself what a load of hooey all this face stuff was.

I took the drive on the left, ducking my head the whole time, even though I didn't need to by a long shot. I kept walking, unravelling the string as I went and keeping an ear out for the slide of a snake.

Well, I knew these drives pretty well, but after a bit I found a new tunnel on my left which I hadn't ever been in before. There was a strange monkey in the left wall. And a monkey isn't a thing that swings through the trees but the word we miners use for a sort of a hole. And I figured it must be where Dad had been jackhammering recently, because he had left his pick there. Well, there was a smell of some kind which I'd never smelt here before. I reckoned it might just be the smell you get at night down an opal drive, because I'd never been out in one at night like this. Anyway, I went through the monkey and as far as I could go along the new drive.

Well, right in this corner I waved the torch around until I suddenly saw something pretty unusual. There was a massive heap of rubble in the corner. It wasn't just opal dirt and tailings. Oh no, it seemed like the whole part of the roof had collapsed and fallen in like a big mushroom. The first thing I thought was: "Shit, that means some more of the roof might fall down on top of me." I turned to follow my string back to the ladder, thinking that the last thing my family needed right now was a squashed Ashmol, when suddenly I had this peculiar kind of mind-flash which made me freeze in my tracks. I said to myself: "What if Pobby and Dingan got caught under the pile of rock?" And then I listened carefully and sort of convinced myself that I could hear a little moaning and breathing. And then I, Ashmol Williamson, found myself calling their names. I really did. "Pobby! Dingan! Don't worry, Ashmol is here! Kellyanne's brother! Pobby and Dingan! I'm here to rescue you." But then I remembered that Kellyanne was convinced they were dead, and that meant they probably were. And so I took off the stones more slowly and didn't hurry so much. But I was so excited I could have filled up a bucket with my sweat and sent it up on the hoist.

I set about on hands and knees taking off rocks and moving them to one side until I got to the floor. And there suddenly, right in front of me, was the wrapper of a Violet Crumble chocolate bar. And it was just great to see something a little familiar with those good old words written on it way out here in the middle of nowhere. But then suddenly my eye caught hold of something else flashing up at me. Something sitting there in the dark. Waiting. A sort of greeny-red glint. I headed straight for it. It was a nobbie the size of a yo-yo, and when I shone my torch on it I could see there was a bit of colour there. My heart beat the world record for the pole vault. I brushed the dirt off as best I could and then I licked the nobbie. It was opal. Green. Red. Black. All of them together. It was strangely warm, like it had already been in someone's hand or close to someone's skin. I sat there for a while, my heart doing a back flip, thinking: "Shit, we Williamsons are going to be rich bastards!" I rolled it around in my palm and licked the dirt off again to make it shine. And I reckoned the opalized bit was as bright as a star and the size of a coin, or a bellybutton. And that gave me the idea. This was Dingan's bellybutton. This was Pobby and Dingan, who got trapped under the roof of the drive where it fell in. And the smell I smelt earlier was death. And the last thing they ate before they died was a Violet Crumble. Everything sort of fit together perfectly.

I put the nobbie in my shoe and the Violet Crumble wrapper in my pocket, and my torch in my mouth, and took up the bodies of Pobby and Dingan in my arms. They were heavier than I'd thought. Much, much heavier. I made my way back along the drive towards the foot of the ladder, the torch moving along the browny-red walls. And I found myself groaning and muttering as I dragged Pobby and Dingan back. There was something heavy about the air too, if you know what I mean.

At the foot of the ladder I paused and set Pobby and Dingan down gently, remembering that there was no way a little bloke like me was going to get them up to the top all by myself. So I laid them both down and took off my coat and draped it over them. As I climbed up the ladder I kept looking back down over my shoulder to make sure the corpses were still at the bottom. And then I got back on my Chopper and pedalled back home under a sky which was still laid up with opal-fever. I was colder than any cold thing a bloke could think of.

# 10

I didn't sleep the rest of that long night, but when the morning finally showed up I walked into Kellyanne's room to tell her what had happened. Everything smelt a bit of sick. I shook Kellyanne on the shoulder and said, "Wake up, Sis. I've got to show you something. Wake up!" Kellyanne's eyelids fluttered and her eye peeped out. She looked like she didn't have much life left in her. I felt sort of desperate. It was going to be me against death. Me on my own. Not James Blond, not Luke Skywalker or nobody, but just Ashmol Williamson speaking to save his sister's life. I'd seen Fat Walt and the legendary Domingo and Joe Lucas and all those others fail. I kind of knew this was my last chance and so I took a real deep breath.

"I did what you said, Kellyanne—I went down the mine last night—and guess what—the roof had collapsed in one of the drives—Pobby and Dingan got caught under it—I know it because I found the opal that

Dingan wore in her bellybutton—they were lying all bruised in the mine—they were—honest—they were there—and they were dead. But they looked peaceful, like—they were lying together holding hands—and they were still a little warm and everything."

Tears started coming out of my eyes, maybe cos I was knackered, but also because I was damn worried that Kellyanne wasn't going to believe a word of what I was saying. I was afraid that if I stopped talking she would suddenly turn and say, "Stop being a drongo, Ashmol. That wasn't Pobby and Dingan," so I just sort of spouted everything out in a big blabber. "They had their eyes closed, Kellyanne—in Pobby's hand was a Violet Crumble wrapper." I waved the wrapper around while I was talking to try and get her attention. "You can see for youself, Sis—I left the bodies laid out at the claim, under my coat—because I couldn't lift them— see—and if you come with me I'll show you. But you gotta believe me—they were there—I lifted off the rocks and I could smell them—no kidding—the roof came down on top of them—there were no props or pillars—it came down and squashed them—honest—I dragged them back to the ladder—but I couldn't get 'em up—I really couldn't."

Well, then I looked at the floor and sort of rubbed my ankles together, and cracked the joints in my fingers.

"Can I see the opal?" Kellyanne whispered after a while.

I took off my shoe and held out the opal in the palm of my hand, which was shaking like a fish. I suddenly got really worried, because I thought: "This opal doesn't look like nothing anyone would put in their bellybutton." It was too big.

But Kellyanne sat up suddenly and put her arms around my neck and said: "Ashmol! You've found the bodies. You've found Pobby and Dingan! This is it! This is the stone that Dingan wears in her bellybutton!"

When I heard this I was suddenly all unplugged and relieved and excited. This huge smile had taken hold of Kellyanne's face. It was like a big rock had been lifted off her. I suddenly thought: "Great! It's all over! I've done it! Now Kellyanne will get better and everything's going to be fine."

But Kellyanne looked at me and said: "Now all you've got to do, Ashmol, is arrange the funeral."

"What?" I thought for a minute she was talking about her own funeral.

"All people have funerals. And so must Pobby and Dingan. I can't relax until they're buried, Ashmol. I'd do it myself, but I can't because I have to go to the hospital in Walgett for a few days."

She looked at me again with those tired eyes. I wasn't too sure the hospital would be able to get rid of the dark rings around them.

"You can pay for it with the bellybutton," she said. "That's what Dingan would have wanted. That's what she always said. 'When I die,' she said, 'pay for my funeral with my bellybutton stone.'"

"How much does a funeral cost?"

"A fortune, I think, " Kellyanne replied. "But the opal should just about cover it."

My heart sank when I heard this. I never knew death was so expensive. I had reckoned on buying a new house and getting my mum an air ticket for a holiday in England, and all kinds of other stuff, with the money from that opal. But I made up my mind there and then that the most important thing was getting Kellyanne well again, and if that meant trading an amazing opal for a grave for Pobby and Dingan, then that was what I was going to do.

"I'll only do it if you get better and stop worrying the hell out of Mum and Dad," I said, all firm. "And only if you promise not to go dying, because then I'll have another funeral to arrange and that's going to be a real chore."

"I promise," said Kellyanne. "Thanks, Ashmol. And now you promise me something too. Promise you won't tell Mum and Dad about finding Dingan's opal."

"Okay. Okay."

"And that you won't go showing it to anyone except the funeral director."

"I promise."

"And don't go trying to get any money for it. This isn't your opal, and it's not Dad's opal either, Ashmol.

This is Dingan's bellybutton. It isn't some ordinary stone you can go making a heap of money from."

I thought about this long and hard, and I thought what a shame it was that I was going to be giving away my first red-on-black. And then I said:

"I promise not to go making any money on it." And then I left the room, almost worn out with promising.

## 11

So the next day, after Mum and Dad had gone off with Kellyanne to take her to the hospital, I walked out on the road that goes past the golf course and out to the cemetery. I walked past the sign which says *Lightning Ridge Population—?* And the question mark is there cos of all the people who pass through, find nothing and give up and go back home. And because of all the folks out hidden at their mines in the bush. And all the criminals and that who don't care to register themselves down on the electoral roll. My mum said she reckoned there were around eight thousand and fifty-three plus Pobby and Dingan, that's eight thousand and fifty-five residents out at the Ridge all together. But now Pobby and Dingan were dead I guess it was back to eight thousand and fifty-three.

As I walked I turned Dingan's bellybutton around in my fingers. I had been so busy I hadn't had a hell of a lot of time to look at it. It was pretty incredible. A mixture of black and greens, and when you turned it a flash of red went shivering through it from side to side. And it was wrapped up cosy in a doona of white-and-brown rock. It had good luck written all over it, that's for sure. And it was warm from the Lightning Ridge sun.

I finally got to the cemetery and I had a good look around. I'd never been there before. It's a small, quiet place not far at all from some mines and about the size of two claims strung together. If you look hard you can see the tops of drilling rigs peeking over the trees like dinosaurs or skeletons of giraffes. Well, you could tell which ones of the dead people had struck opal and which hadn't, because some of the signs were cut out of stone and marble, and some were just two bits of rotting wood crossed over. Kellyanne was right. Death looked like it was just too expensive for some people. Plus it was weird thinking of all those dead people under the ground, especially when you thought about how a lot of the dead folks had spent their lives working under the ground as well. Many of the signs said *Killed in Mining Accident*. And there were flowers and colourful stones under their names and most of them said R.I.P. I used to think that meant they'd sort of been ripped out of their lives like opal ripped out of the clay.

I noticed that Bob the Swede had a bit of space next to his grave. Room enough for two more, I thought, if old Bobby-boy budged over a bit. There was graves for little kids who died young as well. They were under piles of earth like the mullock heaps out at the mines, only reddy-brown. I suddenly felt mighty sad about Kellyanne and I was thinking what it might be like if she had to be buried out here in a sad little grave with a few plastic flowers in front, and all because a couple of imaginary friends died out in my dad's mine. But I told myself to stop thinking like this, and that everything was going to be okay now, because I'd managed by some fluke to find the bodies. She'd get better once she'd mourned at the funeral I was going to buy with Dingan's bellybutton stone. There were tears in my eyes, but. Maybe it was cos I had to get rid of my first opal. Anyway, I think it was only the second time I ever had them in my whole life.

# 12

I knocked on the door of Mr. Dan Dunkley, the funeral
director. A voice said, "Come in." I turned the handle
of his door and entered.

Mr. Dan was a fat man with too many chins for his
own good. His office was spick-and span—well, spick,
anyway—and he was sitting at his desk with his cheek
in his flabby white hand. Behind him he had a grinding
wheel going and a couple of dibbers and dob-sticks laid
out on a tray next to a bottle of methylated spirits and a
Little Dixie Combination Assembly. On his forehead
Mr. Dan had his weird glasses for looking at opals. Like
most people out at the Ridge who don't have the guts to
mine, he did a bit of cutting and buying and selling on
the side to keep him ticking over when not enough
people were kicking the bucket.

Mr. Dan looked up at me. He didn't know who I was,
unlike most people, and my guess is he wasn't too socia-
ble and only got to know people when they had croaked

it. I said: "My name is Ashmol Williamson and I have come to talk graves."

Mr. Dan took off his specs and did a frown and lit up his pipe. After a while he muttered: "School project?"

"No sir," I said. "You may have heard about my sister Kellyanne Williamson? She's dying."

Well, I figured he was bound to twig when I told him Kellyanne's name. He probably had her coffin all ready and made up out back. Sure enough, a bit of a nod came up on his face.

"Reason she's dying is she lost two of her friends a while back. And she's sad," I said.

"Oh," said Mr. Dan. "I didn't know that. All I know about you Williamsons is that your daddy's in a spot of trouble."

I walked over and bunked myself up onto Mr. Dunkley's desk and sat there like a cat, looking at him. "These friends of my sister," I said, "they went missing. They were gone a few days and nobody could find them."

Mr. Dan suddenly looked interested. "I didn't know any of this."

"Well. You're the only one who doesn't," I said. "See. That's the reason you ain't had too many people coming in with opals to sell recently. Everybody's been out looking for Pobby and Dingan all day long. Nobody's been mining."

"Are you sure you ain't making this up, kid?"

"Positive," I said, all confident and smart, like James Blond.

Mr. Dan walked over and switched the grinding wheel off.

"Well, boy, what do you want me to do? Go looking for two kids down a hole? Happens all the time, little fella. Kids don't take any notice of where they're going, cos they got their heads in the clouds, and then they trip up and fall. Wham! Splat!" Mr. Dan whopped his hand down hard on his desk.

There was a silence, and then I looked at him and said, "There's no point in going looking for them, Mr. Dan. I don't want you to do that. The thing is, these two friends of my sister's, they are sort of imaginary. They don't exist. They's invisible. And besides, I've found them, or found their bodies at any rate. They're dead."

Mr. Dan almost choked on his pipe. He sighed and said, "Listen, kid. Ashley, or whatever you're called. I'm a busy bloke. Now hop it."

"I noticed there is a space next to Bob the Swede in the cemetery," I said, refusing to budge.

Mr. Dan took the glasses off his forehead. "You been playin' around in my cemetery, kid?"

I didn't see how he could claim it was his cemetery. The dead owned it. It was their claim. Or else they were ratting it under his nose.

"I wanna buy that space for a grave for Pobby and Dingan," I told Mr. Dan. "You see, I don't think my sis is going to get better until she sees them buried once and for all."

"You can't bury imaginary people," said Mr. Dan. "There's nothing to bury."

"Believe what you want, Mr. Dan," I answered. "Just let me buy the claim. Let me have a space in the cemetery."

"What you offering?"

"Opal." I took off my right shoe and fished out Dingan's bellybutton. I had chipped off all the dirt and polished it up with a cloth so it looked better than ever. So beautiful and sparkling. My fingers didn't like handing it over. Mr. Dan Dunkley took it in his big hand and held it under his light. I was all twitchy and I never took my eyes off it once.

"Fuck me dead!" he said. "Where d'you get this, kid? You rat this? You better not have ratted this. Where d'you get it?" I never saw anyone put on his opal-glasses so quick.

"Noodling."

"You found this noodling?"

"Yup. Noodling on a mullock heap at my dad's claim."

"This don't look like no opal some kid found noodling on his dad's mullock heap. I reckon you ratted it from Old Sid."

I started getting a bit pissed at this. I suppose I was beginning to feel like Kellyanne and Dad. It wasn't too cool having folks not believing what you were saying all the time.

"I bloody well did not," I said.

"This is a valuable stone. This is worth a lot of money, kid," said Mr. Dan.

"Is it worth as much as a grave and a couple of coffins?" I asked him.

Mr. Dan sharpened up his eyes and looked me up and down. He leant closer over his desk.

"Just about," he said in a whisper. "Your daddy know about this, son?"

"Nope. And I don't want him to. Because if he knew about it, Mr. Dan, then he'd go crazy with excitement and then he wouldn't let me buy Pobby and Dingan a grave with it, and then Kellyanne wouldn't get any better."

"Anybody else know?"

"Nobody 'cept Kellyanne."

Dan Dunkley held the stone under the light again and twisted it around so the red flash streaked across it. I could see those colours coming up beautiful and I knew I was on to a winner.

"Okay, son. You got a deal," said Mr. Dan. "I'll let you have the grave for the opal."

"Great!" I said. "And I want you to arrange the funeral for Pobby and Dingan too, Mr. Dan," I said. "And make it realistic. My sis won't get better if it's not realistic. You better make it like a funeral for two normal kids and make them coffins and everything and read some Bible stuff. Make it on Sunday at eleven."

"I'll talk to the preacher," said Mr. Dan, not taking his eyes off Dingan's bellybutton stone. "And you'd better talk to him too. He's gonna think I'm doolally or something."

# 13

I walked out of Dan Dunkley's house a little dazed. I was pleased I'd got a space for Pobby and Dingan in the cemetery, but I had a hollow, aching feeling behind my ribs which wouldn't go away. I couldn't believe an opal had passed through my hands so quick. An opal I had found on my lonesome on the Williamsons' claim at Wyoming. I felt like I was living in a dream or something. Everything was moving so fast.

The preacher was a small weedy man drinking beer from a green bottle on the stump of a sandalwood tree around the back of his pokey white church. I told him what was what. After a long pause he looked at me and said, "Okay, I'll do it, young Ashmol. Now you'd better give me some hard facts about these little imaginary friends, so I can make me a speech."

I thought about it long and hard. Eventually I said: "Well, vicar, they was quiet and they always went around together. And they liked chewing lollies, and Violet Crumbles and Cherry Ripes."

The preacher noted these things down on his pad. He repeated the words "Violet Crumbles" and "Cherry Ripes."

"And they used to go and bathe at the Bore Baths with Kellyanne."

And then I reeled off a sort of list of all the things I had learnt about Pobby and Dingan:

Pobby was a boy and the oldest by a year.

Dingan was the pretty one. Real pretty. And smart as a fox.

They didn't leave no footprints because they walked in the same place as Kellyanne.

And Pobby and Dingan weren't scared of the big kids in Lightning Ridge.

And Dingan read books over your shoulder.

And Pobby liked going out to dance in the lightning storms.

And Dingan could run real quick and play rigaragaroo.

And they liked Kellyanne better than anyone else.

And Pobby had a kind of limp, and when Kellyanne was late for anything she always said Pobby slowed her up and she was late because she had to wait for him.

And Pobby could walk through walls.

The preacher made some more jottings and I saw him running out of page.

> And Dingan had an opal in her belly-button.
> And Kellyanne always sat in between
> Pobby and Dingan on the bus to
> Walgett.
> And Dingan was a pacifist, because every
> time I stamped on her or punched her and
> said, "If Dingan is real why doesn't she hit
> back?" Kellyanne would say, "Cos Dingan is
> a pacifist, stupid."
> And they was generous, because Kellyanne
> was always thanking them for being nice
> to her.
> And they talked English or whistled to make
> themselves understood.
> And you had to be a certain kind of person
> to hear them.

The preacher had stopped writing and was staring into space. "Thanks, Ashmol," he said. "That's plenty of information. Now, take care of your sister, and I'll see you on Sunday."

"Will Pobby and Dingan go to heaven or hell, vicar?" I asked before I went. I was sort of testing him out to see if he'd take Kellyanne's friends seriously.

The preacher thought long and hard about this and said: "What do *you* think?"

"Heaven," I said firmly, "so long as there's Violet Crumbles there."

"I think you're right," said the preacher and took another swig out of his green bottle. As I rode off on my Chopper he shouted: "I shall be praying for your father, Ashmol Williamson!"

"Do what you want, vicar!" I called back. "Just come up with the goods."

I zoomed off down the road thinking about heaven. It was like the ballroom of an opal mine. Full of people with lamps on their heads. And everyone was singing Elvis Presley songs and gouging, and swinging picks.

# *14*

Before I got home I stopped off at Humph's Moozeum, which is a place full of amazing junk. The Moozeum is just down from the half-built castle which the bloke Domingo who I told you about was building single-handed out there in the middle of nowhere. That's Lightning Ridge for you. People go all weird on you all the time, because it's so hot, and they start building castles and shit.

The man who owns the Moozeum is called Humph and he has spent his whole life collecting weird things. Well, I liked to stop by and talk to him sometimes, and when I was sad it was a good place to go to cheer yourself up and get your mind on something else. There is a whole load of outhouses and old buses and cars and bits of mining machinery, and bush fridges, and there is a whole assortment of objects, old pictures, bones, bottles, books, sewing machines. There's a car up a tree, and Humph even has the toes of one of his miner-friends pickled in a jar. He is getting some bloke's leg pickled too. He has a chunk of fossilized Turkish Delight from Gallipoli, and a bottle of vodka which he says a band called the Rolling Stones gave him. He is a clever old bugger, Humph. You never know if what he is saying is true.

One of the sections of the Moozeum is underground, and that's where I found old Humph sitting at the little bar he has in the corner. He was wearing a big floppy hat. "Ah, Ashmol," he said. "Any news of Pobby and Dingan yet? Bit like looking for a needle in a haystack, I reckon."

"Yeah, I found them," I told him proudly. "They were both dead."

Old Humph didn't know whether to say "Good" or "That's too bad" and so he just grunted and held up something to show me. I trundled over and stood looking. I was pretty impressed. It was a framed invitation to the funeral of Princess Diana. And the writing was done in really fancy silver lettering and there was a royal stamp on it and everything. "You got invited to the funeral of Princess Diana?" I asked with my eyes wide open.

"Did I hell!" said Humph, fairly splitting his sides with laughter. "This little bewdy I cut out of a magazine and stuck down on a piece of card! Don't tell anyone, mind. The tourists love it." That was Humph. He was a cunning old-timer who didn't care too much about the truth of things so long as there was a good story in it,

and most of the time he told people about his fakes anyway, so they could see how clever he'd been.

"Could you do me some invitations for Pobby and
Dingan's funeral?" I asked.

"Having a funeral, are you?"

I nodded. "I reckon Kellyanne won't get better until
we bury the dead bodies and show them some last
respect."

Humph nodded solemnly. "I wouldn't have minded
having their dead bodies in my Moozeum," he said. "I
haven't got any dead imaginary friends in my Moozeum
yet. 'Bout the only thing I haven't got."

"Maybe Kellyanne will let you get Pobby's finger
pickled and put in a jar," I suggested.

"Maybe," said Humph, taking a swig of Johnnie
Walker. "So how many invitations do you want?"

"I want to invite everyone in Lightning Ridge."

Humph nodded solemnly and scratched the top of
his floppy hat.

"That makes eight thousand and fifty-three by my
calculation," I said.

# 15

The day of Dad's trial arrived. I wasn't allowed to go to the magistrate's court, so I can't say exactly what happened. I can only imagine it. But the fat and the thin of it was that, after he'd finished punishing someone for breaking and entering and when he had fined John the Gun and some other blokes for shooting too many roos, Judge McNulty made Dad stand up and tell the little jury about what he was doing out at Old Sid's mine that evening.

Well, this time my dad didn't make up a lost-cat story or make out he was just looking for his contact lenses. No way. He stood up straight and told them that he was out looking for Pobby and Dingan, the imaginary friends of his daughter Kellyanne Williamson, and that he was just checking to see if they'd wandered over onto Old Sid's claim. And Mum said Judge McNulty looked all confused, like a jigsaw puzzle before you put it together, and that he asked Dad to describe their appearance. I flinched a bit as I imagined my old man stuttering and tongue-twistering as he tried to get to grips with that one. Well, my dad must have handled it pretty well, but, because then McNulty moved straight on and asked whether Dad was on any drugs, and whether Dad thought the imaginary friends really existed. And apparently Dad looked old McNulty and the jury and everybody dead straight with his opal eyes and said that at first he thought they didn't exist, and then he wasn't too sure about it, and now he was positive they did exist after all, because he was on trial for ratting because of them and he was a little angry with them for it too.

Judge McNulty rubbed his chin and scratched his head a lot. And then Old Sid, that whiskery bastard—as Mum called him—got up with a bandage over his nose and testified and called my father "mentally deranged" and lots of other things, including a "low-down piece of roo shit." And some of Old Sid's miner-mates backed him up and talked a lot about how much my dad would drink and how he was always interested in other people's opal and where they had found it. And that confirmed he was a ratter as far as they could see. And then a policeman said how he saw Dad snotting Sid in the nose, only he didn't say "snotting."

Well, according to Mum, the judge fidgeted around and whispered things to people. And then McNulty looked at the little jury and told them that the whole question of Mr. Rex Williamson's guilt depended on

whether it should be considered a crime to hit someone
on the nose when they have called you a ratter and also
on whether the jury believed he was really out looking
for his daughter's imaginary friends that night. And he
told the jury that meant they needed to work out for
themselves how real they thought Pobby and Dingan
were.

And Mum said you could see the jury mulling it over,
and whispering the names Pobby and Dingan over
plenty, and she reckoned that most of them were thinking, "Since half the town has been out looking for
Pobby and Dingan, why couldn't it just be possible that
the father of Kellyanne Williamson was looking as
well?" And then the jury heard from my dad that a
funeral of Pobby and Dingan was taking place the next
day, organized by his son Ashmol Williamson, and if
the judge wanted he and the jury could come along and
see what real people they had been. And then Old Sid
and his lawyer complained that the funeral had been
dreamt up to distract from Rex Williamson's crime and
that Pobby and Dingan were just invented on the spot as
a sort of cover-up.

Mum told me that then Judge McNulty did lots of
racking of his brains, and sometimes he looked a bit
pale, but eventually he decided to break up the court
until it was possible to interview Kellyanne. But he only
did it after asking Sid about his family. And Sid said he
hadn't got any, and that his wife had died twenty years
ago. And the judge asked him if he ever talked to her

privately even though she was dead. And Sid said he did sometimes, when he was up at the agitator, because his wife used to help him sift through opal dirt because she had better eyes than he did. But I don't think Sid realized what was going on, that the sly old Judge McNulty had trapped him into admitting that everybody has an imaginary friend of some kind even if you don't think they have, and that Old Sid himself was a bit on the short-sighted side.

After that, McNulty announced that the court was going to come together again when Kellyanne was better. And at the end of the proceedings only about twenty or thirty people were outside the courtroom to throw cabbages and things at my dad and hiss: "Ratter. Ratter. Ratter. Ratter." And only one bloke had a banner saying POBBY AND DINGAN WERE RATTERS on it in red paint like blood.

# 16

Well, to be honest, all this trial stuff cheered me up no end, and the next day Mum and me got ready for the funeral of Pobby and Dingan with smiles on our faces while Dad went off to fetch Kellyanne from the hospital.

Mum had bought me some new black pants and a black sweatshirt, and so we went out all comfortably to the cemetery and decorated the fence with flowers and opened up the gate. And the priest came and talked things through with us, you know, about what the proceedings were. And Mr. Dan drove up around ten o'clock and shuffled around a little awkward in his suit and tie. And then the coffins of Pobby and Dingan turned up and I helped carry them up to the grave. And old Humph came along in his hat to tell me he was putting a plaque for Pobby and Dingan up in his Moozeum. Well, I was looking forward to telling Kellyanne this when she arrived from the hospital with

Dad. That would put a massive smile on her face, for sure. And she would never be sick again.

And then all that was left to do was to wait for people to start arriving. I had some butterflies in my stomach, but. You see, I'd been round the whole of Lightning Ridge posting Humph's invitations into everybody's mailboxes. And I was sort of nervous to see how many came and how many tore up the invitations and still called us Williamsons a bunch of frigging lunatics. And I was also nervous because of the reports about Kellyanne and how she was getting worse by the day even though they'd managed to pump some food into her at the hospital. So it seemed pretty much like it was now or never.

I got so afraid that people wouldn't turn up and that I might have to imagine myself a whole crowd that I got really impatient, and an hour before the funeral was due to start I got on my bike again and went pedalling around Lightning Ridge to see if people were getting ready. The place was a sort of deathly quiet. I sat on the step outside The Digger's Rest for half an hour, trembling and half wanting to go for a piss.

Eventually a few people started stepping out of houses and shops coughing, or pulling back curtains and doors. And then suddenly, as the sun got hotter in the sky, old buggers, young buggers, men and women and dogs started appearing on the street and walking out towards the cemetery. A couple of them saw me and waved. I got on my Chopper fast and cycled around the back way, standing up on the pedals to get a good view of the crowd walking along in silence between the gum trees and houses. And I noticed that everyone had like made an effort and changed out of their mining clothes into their best boardies and singlets.

I got back to the cemetery ahead of the people and I saw them all coming up the road past the balding little golf course like a massive great wave. I stood on Bob the Swede's gravestone and saw that actually there were many more than I'd expected. Thousands of people all coming out towards us. More even than you saw at the goat races, more even than I'd ever seen in my whole life except on the football on TV. And for a moment I was worried that there was something else going on that they were all going to, and that they were going to walk straight past the cemetery gates or something and head out of town.

But I shouldn't have worried, because pretty soon the little cemetery was full of living people, and everyone closed in around the grave and the coffins which had Pobby and Dingan inside. And some sat on the scorched grass, and some wandered around looking at some of the other graves. And no one was saying nothing except a few words to each other. But most just gave me a nod and gazed out over the land or fanned themselves down. And Mum and me had made some lemonade and cookies earlier, and so we passed some cups around and began pouring, so that people had something to graze on. But although I was relieved to see all these people turn up at the cemetery for the funeral of Pobby and Dingan, the most important ones hadn't arrived. And that was Kellyanne and Dad.

Kellyanne and Dad. Dad and Kellyanne. They still hadn't come back from the hospital. It was way past time for the funeral to start and people were starting to do a bit of muttering and all that. And I suppose some of them were starting to doubt if there was going to be a funeral at all. And perhaps some folks were beginning to look at each other and at me and my mum and starting to ask each other what the hell they were doing attending the funeral of two figments of a girl's imagination, especially when that little girl wasn't even there. And I remember picking out Judge McNulty in the crowd. He was frowning and looking at his watch. But at least the preacher was doing a good job. He was pretty sober and he was still going around welcoming people and saying hello and handing out sheets with some songs printed on them. I reckon he wasn't keen to lose all these people. Because if they stayed it would be the biggest congregation he ever preached to in his life. At one moment he looked up and gave me a thumbs-up sign as if to say: "Don't worry, mate, Kellyanne will be here soon."

And then suddenly she came. I recognized the sound of the ute as it came in the gate, and there was Dad at the wheel. And everyone turned around and stood watching as he climbed out and walked to the back and began to take out a fold-up wheelchair and assemble it on the grass. I ran down to meet him. Through the back window I could see Kellyanne's pale face. I ran to the back door and opened it and Kellyanne turned and gave me a twitch—because she had no strength for a whole smile. She was as thin as I have ever seen a person get, and Mum came and helped me lift her into the wheelchair which Dad had assembled. And there were tears in Mum's eyes and the funeral hadn't even started. Well, then Mum gave Dad a big hug and a kiss right on the lips and I did a yuck sign to Kellyanne by sticking my finger down my throat, and then I pushed Kellyanne up the slope through the crowd and up to the grave of Pobby and Dingan. And most people I think were pretty shocked to see my sister looking so sick. And some of them said nice things to her on the way up, like "Good on yer, gal," and "She's a brave one." And somebody else's mum put flowers on her lap. And then, when she got to the top, everyone suddenly started clapping and everyone was cheering and people were slapping my dad on the back. It took a fair while for everyone to settle down and listen to the preacher, who was now standing up at the front and looking like he wanted to speak.

He shouted out: "G-day, everybody! And welcome to the funeral of Pobby and Dingan, friends of Kellyanne Williamson and members of the good honest Williamson family!" Well, at that point Humph let out a huge cheer, but he was the only one and I think he felt a bit of a drongo for doing it. But my dad had a little smile to himself. And then the preacher told us we were going to sing from our song sheets and everyone rustled their papers.

Well, Kellyanne had chosen the songs, and first we sang the Australian National Anthem, "Australians all let us rejoice for we are young and free," and all that, and then Fingers Bill played a Cat Stevens song on his guitar and those who didn't know the words sort of just hummed it, and it went "Oooh baby it's a wide world," or something like that. And Kellyanne had chosen it because it was Pobby and Dingan's favourite song. And it was quite amazing hearing all these people singing together. And I wouldn't say it was too tuneful or anything like that. But it was loud as hell and I reckon the emus out on the Moree Road didn't have no trouble hearing it.

Well, then the preacher coughed and took out a piece of paper and said: "I would now like to say a few words about the deceased." And this is how his speech went:

*People of Lightning Ridge, g-day. We have come together here today to celebrate the lives of Pobby and Dingan, two close mates of Kellyanne Williamson. They have brought much pleasure to our hearts and what a sad loss it is to say our final goodbyes to them—whom many of us never even saw, but only felt. We recall with pleasure Dingan's calm pacifist nature, her opal bellybutton and her pretty face, and many of us will remember Pobby's limp and his generous heart, and let us give thanks for their lives, which, whatever anyone says, they most certainly lived.*

Well, people were sniffing and taking out handkerchiefs already. And even some of those real legend, tough miners were weeping onto the backs of their hands, and taking out rags covered in dirt to blow their noses into. The preacher raised his hand and pointed out at the crowd. He turned up the volume on his voice:

*And there are some of you here today who have not believed! You have not believed in the invisible, because it does not shine forth from the earth and sell for thousands of dollars! And there are many of you here who have not believed in Pobby and Dingan. But God believes in them. And he believes in you. Yup. He sure believes in everyone here. Oh, yes, indeedee. And we are invisible. We are invisible and transparent and shallow and yet God believes in us. And God believes in Pobby and Dingan and he is in every single one of those lollies they sucked and was with them on the school bus, and when they played rigaragaroo and when they danced in the lightning, and even, I tell you, when they went missing so tragically out at the Wyoming claim, where Kellyanne and her brother Ashmol and their honest dad Rex Williamson went looking for them. God was with Pobby and Dingan and is still with them in heaven. Amen.*

Well, thank God the preacher didn't go on for too long after that! He just said some things about Kelly-anne and what a brave girl she was and he said I was a plucky kid for sticking up for Pobby and Dingan and fighting for them to have a proper burial. And there was more clapping and my dad slapped me on the back so hard he almost knocked my teeth out. And then the preacher gave himself a more serious look and shouted out something about how if anyone had any reason why Pobby and Dingan should not be buried in the cemetery for them to step forward and say it now. And there was a long silence and I held my breath. And during the silence I was looking around at all these people trying to fix them with my eyes so they wouldn't budge. But then a bloke called Andy Floom stepped forward and everyone turned and looked at him. And the preacher said, "Well, Andy Floom, speak up!" But Andy Floom, who was a few stubbies short of a six-pack, looked confused and said: "What? Oh, sorry everyone, I was just, like, stepping forward to squash a spider." And people started laughing everywhere. And the preacher said okay, now he'd go on with the burial.

So me and Dad and Mum and a few others got down and lifted the coffins into the grave and Kellyanne watched us silently and totally wide-eyed. And only when we had the coffins all lined up in the dark hole did the preacher say, "Ashes to ashes and dust to dust," and tears start glimmering down her face. And then I pushed Kellyanne forward in her wheelchair and she placed in the grave a whole pack of Cherry Ripes and Violet Crumbles, a couple of books and things. And Mum put in some flowers and then we stood in silence while two miners shovelled in some soil like they did when they filled in a mine shaft that wasn't being used no more. And when the coffins were covered and buried the preacher led a prayer, and after that everybody started walking slowly home, sniffing into their sleeves. And I walked out last, with my dad resting his hand on my shoulder. And on the way out someone stopped us at the gate. It was Old Sid and he was holding out his fists and swaying in the road and shouting: "Come on, Rex Williamson! Come and fight me, you fucking rat-ter! You're not going to get away with this! Turning the whole of the Ridge against me, you piece of shit! You ever come trespassing on my claim again and I'll, I'll, I'll k-kill . . . !" But then some kids ran up to him and started shouting, "Lizard eater! Lizard eater! Old Sid is a lizard eater!" and Sid turned away and we watched them hounding him back up the road as he swiped at them with drunk arms.

Dad and I caught up Mum and Kellyanne on the road. Well, Mum was suddenly smiling and singing out that it was about time we menfolk got back to mining, because she reckoned it wouldn't be too long before we found something. And me and Dad looked at each other and couldn't believe those words came out of her mouth. And as we came up to them, Mum turned the

wheelchair around to show us that Kellyanne was smiling too. And Kellyanne Williamson smiled for the rest
of her life.

But her life was short. A week later the whole population of Lightning Ridge came out to the cemetery
again. My sister Kellyanne Williamson was buried with
her imaginary friends, in the same grave, in the same
place where millions of years ago there had been sea
and creatures swimming cheerfully around. And she
took with her some Violet Crumbles, in case Pobby and
Dingan had run out.

And although in the end everyone believed that
Pobby and Dingan had really lived and were really
dead, nobody at the Ridge could quite believe the
funeral of Kellyanne Williamson was actually happen-
ing. And I, Ashmol, still can't believe that it did. I just
can't. I can't believe it at all. Even now, one year later, it
feels like she's still totally alive. And I find myself lying
awake talking to her all the time. And I talk to her at
school and when I am walking down Opal Street, and
Humph and I when we are out at the Moozeum talk to
her together, and you will still see today if you go to
Lightning Ridge people pause in the middle of doing
whatever they are doing to stop and talk to Kellyanne
Williamson just as they still pause to talk to Pobby and
Dingan and to opal in their dreams. And the rest of the

world thinks we are all total nutters, but they can go and talk to their backsides for all I care. Because they are all just fruit loops who don't know what it is to believe in something which is hard to see, or to keep looking for something which is totally hard to find.

# Acknowledgements

Thanks to Helen and Joe Stratford, Ridge rockhounds. And to Craig Raine, Ian Jack, and the brilliant friends who read drafts: Rich Ager, Lucy Chandler, Helena Echlin, Ben Richardson, David Shelley, Tim Robinson, Philip Traill.

Two publications were a source of information: *The Australian Geographic* and the pamphlet *Miner's Tales from the Black Opal Country* by Rusty Bowen (1997).

Printed in the United States
by Baker & Taylor Publisher Services